THE BUBBLE GUM STORY

Written and Illustrated by Youa Vang

The Bubble Gum Story

Author: Youa Vang
Title: The Bubble Gum Story
written and illustrated by: Youa Vang
For ages pre-school and kindergarten

1st edition

There was a boy named Marty,
who wanted some gum.
He went to the store,
so, he could by some.

"Good Morning Mr. Clerk!
Do you have any gum?
I've waited all day,
so, I could buy some."

"We're all out today.
I cannot sell you some.
Come back tomorrow,
and I will have more gum."

Marty cried, cried and cried.
He did not like that.
He walked home feeling sad,
until he saw his friend Pat.

"Hello there Pat!
I see you're chewing gum.
Is it true? Am I right?
May I please have some?"

"Yes, you are right!
But I will not share my gum.
To the store, you should go!
And there you can buy some."

Marty cried, cried and cried.
He felt sad and unlucky.
He continued walking home,
until he saw his friend Spunky.

"Hello there Spunky!
Is that a bubble from your gum?
Is it true? Am I right?
May I please have some?

"Correct! You are right!
But I will not share my gum.
To the store, you should go!
And there you can buy some.

Marty cried, cried and cried.
He wanted to just grab it.
But he continued walking home,
until he saw his friend Abbot.

"Hello there Abbot!
Can I trouble you for gum.
I've asked all day,
but no one would give me some."

"I dont have anymore.
I ate my last piece of gum.
To the store, you should go!
And there you can buy some."

Marty cried, cried and cried.
He sat on a stump.
He was too sad to walk home,
until he heard Mr. Skump.

"What happened Marty?
I saw you on my way.
Why are you crying,
on this beautiful sunny day?"

"Hello Mr, Skump!
I wanted some gum.
But no one would share.
They would not give me some."

"Do not worry and follow me!
I have plenty of gum.
I deliver to the store,
and I will share more than one."

"Marty was so happy.
He felt very lucky.
He continued walking home,
until he saw Pat, Abbot and Spunky."

"What do you have there?
Is that a bag full of gum?
Is it true? Are we right?
May we please have some?"

"Yes, you are right!
It's a bag full of gum.
To the store, you should all go!
And there you can buy some."

They all cried, cried and cried.
They stood there and stared...

However, Marty is a kind friend,
and so, he turned around and shared.

THE END!

Let's have a gum party!

Author's Bio

Youa Vang is a wife and a mother of four. Although, she is mostly a stay-at-home mom, she and her husband also operate 2 restaurants in the small town of Chico, CA. Youa also runs an online boutique and just recently created her own line of   jewelry. Growing up, her Grandparents would tell   her endless stories from folktales to fairytales. She now tells fictional stories to her kids. Her passion is writing children's book. Now, she can share her stories to all.

Made in the USA
Las Vegas, NV
10 April 2022

47223058R00024